The Wonderful World of Disney

MEGAN

Walt Disney

OLIVER
AND COMPANY

Twin Books

One morning in New York City, some kittens peeked out
from a box on the sidewalk. Passing by, a girl noticed the sign
above the box: "KITTIES NEED HOME." She picked up a
kitten and left. Then a man came by and took another kitten.
Finally, two boys chose two more kittens and a little orange cat
was left alone. The kitten ventured out onto the sidewalk, but
found himself knocked aside by the rushing crowd.

The ginger-colored kitten came upon Louie's hot dog stand. "I'm hungry," he thought, smelling the hot dogs.

Just then, the kitten was startled by Dodger the dog. "Hey, I don't eat cats— too much fur," assured Dodger. "But together we can both have something to eat."

Dodger convinced the hungry kitten to help carry out a plan to get some of Louie's hot dogs. Dodger started barking, chasing the kitten toward the hot dog stand and up Louie's shirt. As Louie yelled and chased the kitten, Dodger grabbed some hot dogs from the cart.

In the meantime, Dodger's friends were watching television in an old abandoned barge at the harbor. "This is boring. Let's see some boxing," whined the chihuahua.

"Shhh. Quiet, Tito," snapped Francis, the bulldog.

"What's keeping him?" asked Rita, who looked like an afghan.

Tito had enough of the program and yanked the cord out. The others were about to clobber little Tito when...

...Dodger showed up with the hot dogs around his neck like a prize medal. "Hey Dodger fans, dinner is served. You should've seen the monster I fought to get this chow."

The kitten had followed Dodger to the harbor, angry that the dog had run off with the sausages. He crept onto the worn-out roof and heard the dogs' voices through a crack.

"Then what happened?" asked the great dane, Einstein, his mouth full of sausage.

"It came toward me, all sharp claws and dripping fangs, and suddenly..."

Just then the ceiling collapsed and the kitten fell with a clatter, scaring the dogs.

The kitten tried to explain himself, "I...I was following this dog..."
"He's lying," Tito snarled.

"I just wanted some of the sausages I helped him get," the kitten said. "That's him—over there."

The gang looked over at Dodger, who was watching television. "Hey kitty, you're late for supper," Dodger said casually.

"Sharp claws, Dodger?" laughed Tito.

"Dripping fangs?" teased Francis.

Tito would have picked a fight with Dodger, but Fagin walked in with a box of dog biscuits. "Sykes will be here any minute," announced Fagin, as he threw some biscuits to the eager dogs.

After the gang devoured the biscuits, they started crowding around their master. "No, no, stop! No, heh, heh..." laughed Fagin.

Soon their play was interrupted by the sound of a car horn. "I'll be right there," called Fagin. He frantically inspected the loot that the gang had brought home that day. "This stuff is worthless, guys! Don't you have anything else?"

All of the dogs cringed. Fagin sighed, "How are we ever going to get out of this one?"

Suddenly, two dobermans burst in, snarling. "Uh...look who's here, kids," said Fagin nervously.

"Nice doggies," said Fagin. He reached out to pet the dobermans, but pulled back in fear as one of them viciously snapped at him. "I was...just on my way out."

After Fagin left, the dobies growled at the gang.

The car lights blinded Fagin as he stumbled to the limousine. He presented the loot to Sykes. "I don't want junk," Sykes said, blowing cigar smoke into Fagin's face. "You have three days to get the cash...or else."

Sykes called back his dogs and drove away.

Back on the barge, the gang was praising the kitten for standing up to one of the dobermans who had attacked him. He had scratched the dog's nose.

Fagin returned and dejectedly collapsed onto his chair. "Three days...I never should have borrowed that money," Fagin whimpered.

The gang tried to comfort Fagin. Tito
put slippers on Fagin's feet. Einstein lifted
up his legs and Dodger slid a crate closer
for a footrest.

Then Fagin recalled, "I saw a cut on one doberman's nose. Who did that?" Dodger gently pushed the kitten toward Fagin.

Fagin cheered up and picked up the little kitten. "You! You!" he laughed. "That took a lot of guts."

"We've never had a cat in the gang before," said Fagin, "but we can use all the help we can get." So the kitten was now a member of Fagin's crew.

The next day the gang went into the city. As planned, Einstein and Francis jumped in front of an oncoming limousine, which screeched to a halt. The driver got out and examined Francis, who pretended to be hurt.

While a crowd gathered around
Francis, Tito and the kitten slipped into
the car to remove the radio.

As Tito was busy with the wires under the dashboard, the
kitten sat atop the dashboard to keep watch. "Tito, there's
someone in the back seat," said the kitten in alarm. He jumped
down and accidentally turned on the ignition.
Tito screamed as a wire zapped him with electricity.

The driver of the limousine, Winston, was holding Francis in his arms when he heard Tito's scream. He ran to the side of the limo in time to see Tito race out of the car.

A girl named Jenny had been sitting in the back seat. When she saw the kitten, she picked him up. "What an adorable kitty!" she said.

"Our cat must still be in the car!" cried Tito. Sure enough, as the limo drove away, the kitten looked back at his friends through the rear window.

"You were supposed to keep an eye on him," Dodger scolded Tito.

"Well, it's hard to watch anything when you're getting fried!" replied Tito.

21

Back at Jenny's home on Fifth Avenue, Jenny prepared some food for the kitten. "I'll take good care of you," she assured him.

"Georgette is not going to like this," Winston mumbled.

Georgette was a purebred poodle, whose prize ribbons were hung on her bedroom wall. Wearing a stylish hairdo and makeup, Georgette entered the kitchen for breakfast. "Cat!" she gasped. "Do you have any idea out of whose bowl you're eating?"

"Uh…yours?" the kitten asked sheepishly.

"Oh, Georgette, this is my new kitty," said Jenny. "I'm going to call him Oliver."

Winston was right. Georgette was not pleased to have Oliver around. "Why should that cat get all the attention?" she complained, seeing Jenny and Oliver at the piano.

"Wait till Mom and Dad return from their trip, Oliver," said Jenny. "They'll love you, too."

"Oh, Jennifer, I don't hear any practicing," Winston called out.

While Jenny played the piano, Oliver plunked some keys. "A duet!" Jenny laughed.

Later that day, Jenny and Oliver went to Central Park. They took a boat ride, chased each other along the fence, and ate ice cream. Then they rode through the park in a carriage. Oliver playfully climbed on top of the carriage and hopped onto Jenny's head. "A new fur hat!" she giggled.

Next, Jenny brought Oliver to a jewelry store. A salesman put a collar around Oliver's neck. It was engraved with his name and Fifth Avenue address.

"Perfect!" said Jenny. Oliver liked the collar, also. It officially declared that he now had a home.

That night Jenny put away her clothes and got into bed. "Good night, Oliver," she said, yawning.

Oliver snuggled up against her under the covers. He had never been so happy.

The next morning the gang waited
across the street as Jenny left for school.
Then Einstein rang the doorbell, and
Francis played dead.

Winston came out and saw the limp
bulldog on the stairs. "You, again!" he
yelled and chased after Francis.

Meanwhile, the rest of the gang rushed
into the house.

The gang looked around in awe. "These paintings are
masterpieces!" said Francis.

"Such fine furniture," remarked Rita, sitting on the sofa.

"And fine food," said Einstein, who had found the kitchen.

Dodger led them upstairs to look for Oliver. They found Georgette lounging on pillows near her bed. They had never seen such a bed—it had drapes and a little stairway. When Georgette saw Dodger, she barked in alarm.

"You're barking up the wrong tree," said Dodger. "We want our cat, not you!"

Georgette gladly led them to Oliver, who was asleep on Jenny's bed. Einstein and Francis swept the kitten into a sack. "Let's hightail outta here!" said Tito.

When the gang returned to the barge at the pier, they unloaded Oliver. "You're home now," said Dodger cheerfully.

"But I...was happy there." Oliver's response surprised the gang.

Just then Fagin arrived. "Only one more day," he brooded. He picked up Oliver and sat down. "Thought you left us, kitty." Then, noticing Oliver's gold tag, Fagin examined it. "1125 Fifth Avenue. So that's where you've been."

Fagin's face brightened. He excitedly walked over to the desk. The gang crowded around him. Fagin wrote: "Dear Mr. Very Rich Cat Owner..."

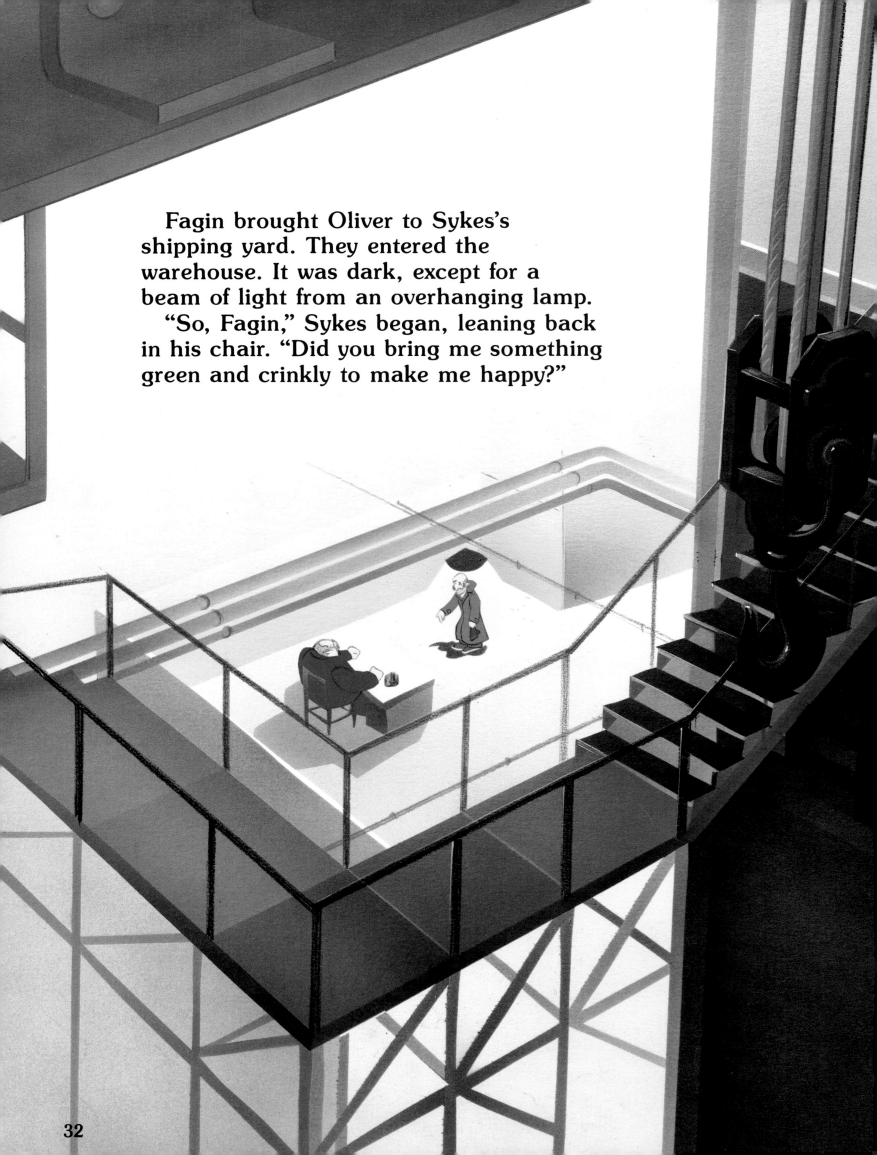

Fagin brought Oliver to Sykes's shipping yard. They entered the warehouse. It was dark, except for a beam of light from an overhanging lamp.

"So, Fagin," Sykes began, leaning back in his chair. "Did you bring me something green and crinkly to make me happy?"

"Sykes, I have an airtight kitty—plan, plan!" Fagin said nervously, putting Oliver on Sykes's desk. He explained how he had kidnapped the cat and left a ransom note. "You'll get your money tonight from this rich family," Fagin said, lifting Oliver's tag for Sykes to read. "They'll meet me at the harbor tonight to get their cat back."

"Well, Fagin," warned Sykes, "this is your last chance."

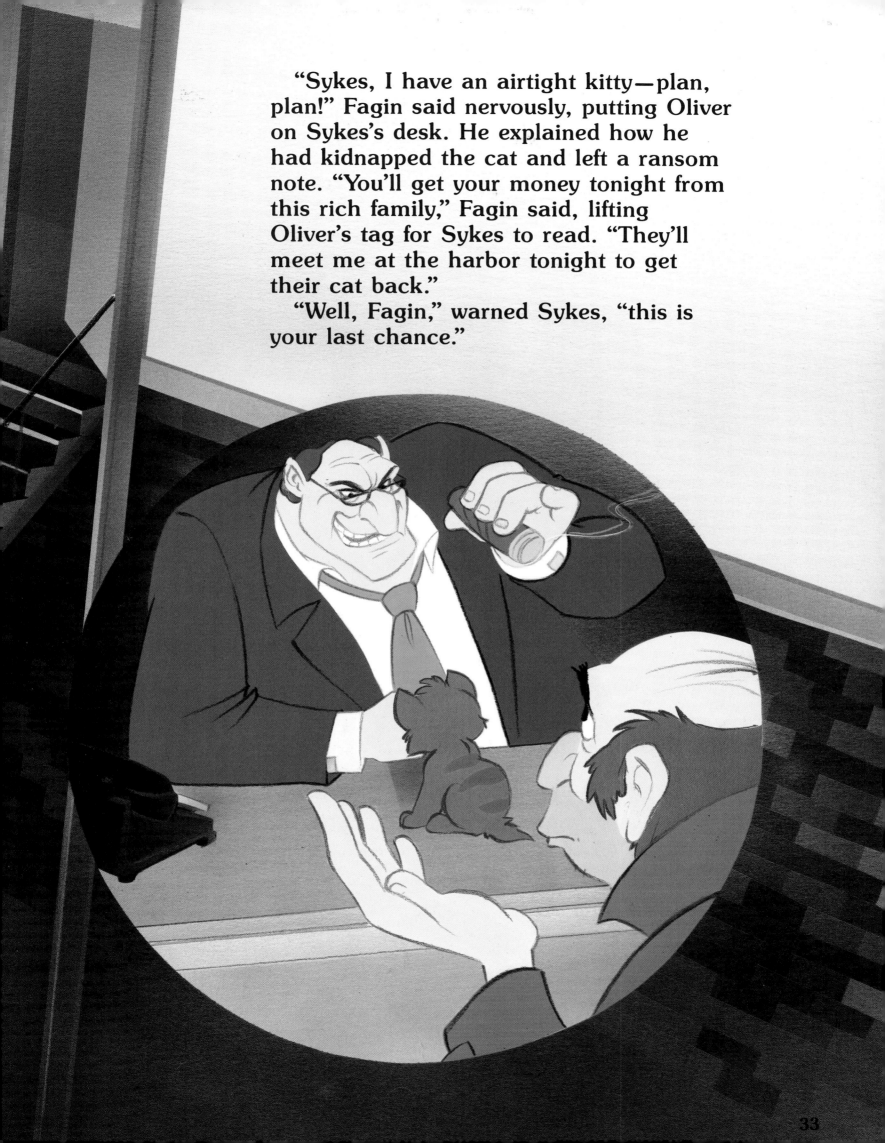

33

While Sykes watched from his parked limo, Fagin anxiously waited for Oliver's owner. Soon Jenny and Georgette appeared. "Excuse me, sir," she said to Fagin. "I'm looking for my stolen kitty. I brought *this* to pay for him." Fagin stared at Jenny's piggy bank and felt awful.

"Isn't that a coincidence?" he said. "I just found a lost kitten. Is he yours?"

"Oh, Oliver!" cried Jenny. "Oh, thank you, mister!"

Suddenly the limousine roared up to them. Sykes pulled Jenny into the car and screeched away. Oliver was left behind.

"You can't do that!" shouted Fagin, running after the limousine.

Inside the barge, the gang heard Jenny's screams and ran out. "Jenny! They took Jenny!" Oliver told them.

"Don't worry, we'll get her back." Dodger winked reassuringly. "After this morning's rescue operation, it'll be a snap."

Sykes had a plan to collect a large ransom fee for the return of Jenny. Back in his office at the warehouse, Sykes tried to call 1125 Fifth Avenue. "What do you mean, it's unlisted!"

As he yelled at the operator, he didn't notice that the gang showed up on the surveillance monitors behind him.

The gang crept along a catwalk and entered the warehouse. While Sykes was on the phone, Einstein quietly locked Sykes's office door.

Meanwhile, the others found Jenny tied to a chair in another room. As they untied her, Sykes's dobermans started barking. "They're coming!" shouted Rita.

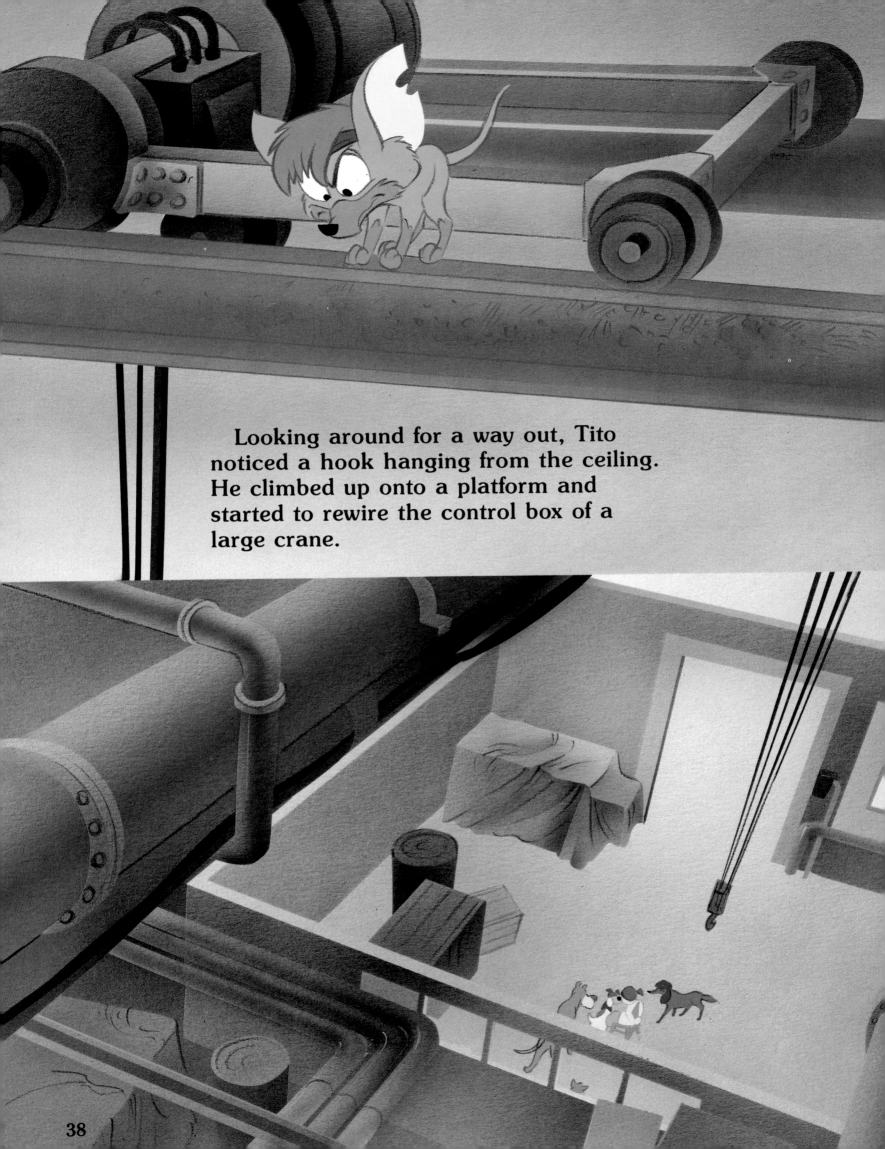

Looking around for a way out, Tito
noticed a hook hanging from the ceiling.
He climbed up onto a platform and
started to rewire the control box of a
large crane.

Dodger attached the hook to Jenny's chair and ordered the gang to climb onto it.

"Quick, Tito!" shouted Dodger.

Just as Oliver climbed onto the chair, the crane started to turn, lifting them up toward the ceiling.

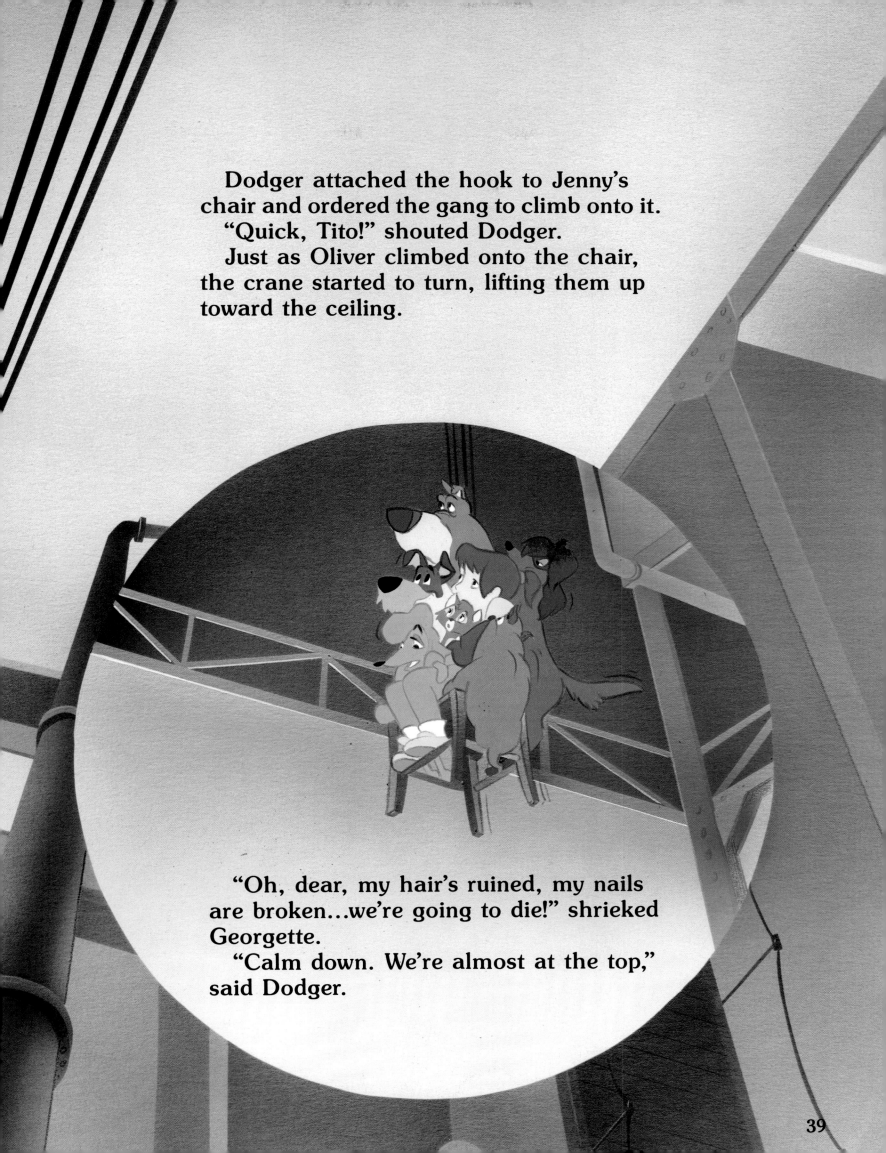

"Oh, dear, my hair's ruined, my nails are broken...we're going to die!" shrieked Georgette.

"Calm down. We're almost at the top," said Dodger.

Just as the gang was hoisted up
through an opening in the ceiling, Sykes
and his dobermans broke into the room.
Sykes grabbed an axe and plunged it into
a control panel.

The surge of electricity threw Tito off
the platform. The crane went dead, and
Jenny and the gang fell in a heap below.

Jenny, the dogs and Oliver quickly
recovered and escaped through a loading
door. On the other side, they were
relieved to see Fagin appear on his three-
wheeled motorcycle.

The gang piled onto the trike and sped away.

Fagin quickly veered down the entrance steps of a subway, and then onto the platform. But to their horror, Sykes's limo bounced down the entrance stairs after them. As they approached the end of the platform, Fagin jumped the trike onto the tracks. Sykes also bounded onto the tracks and closed in on them.

"Help!" screamed Jenny. Sykes rammed the trike, throwing Jenny onto the limo's hood.

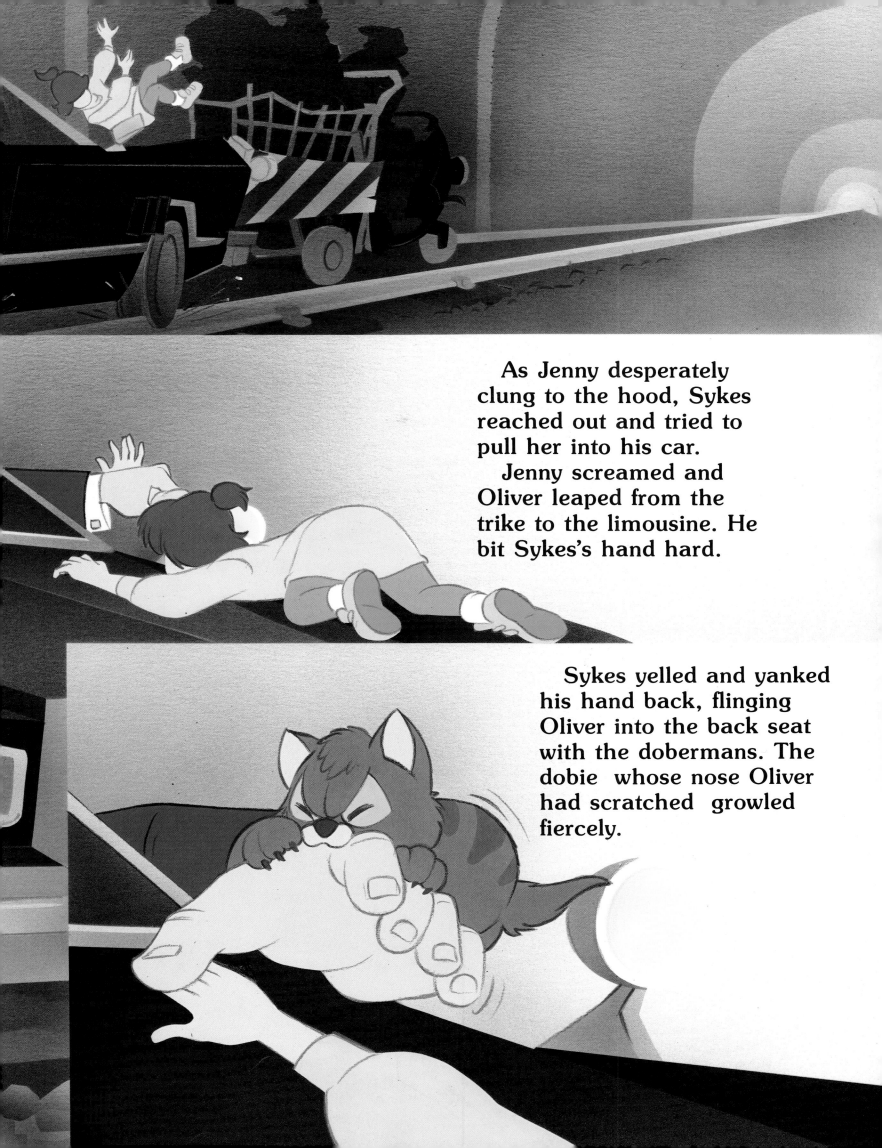

As Jenny desperately clung to the hood, Sykes reached out and tried to pull her into his car.

Jenny screamed and Oliver leaped from the trike to the limousine. He bit Sykes's hand hard.

Sykes yelled and yanked his hand back, flinging Oliver into the back seat with the dobermans. The dobie whose nose Oliver had scratched growled fiercely.

"Mr. Fagin, help!" shrieked Jenny, still clinging to the car. Georgette took over the steering wheel as Fagin pulled Jenny into the trike.

Meanwhile, Dodger jumped into Sykes's car to get Oliver. Dodger lunged at the dobermans, causing them to crash through the rear window. One of the dobies slipped off the hood onto the tracks.

Dodger bravely fought the other doberman.

As the trike and limo swung out onto a bridge, the second dobie slid off the car roof and fell into the river below.

Realizing that the end of the bridge was blocked off, Fagin turned sharply to the right. Sykes slammed on the brakes. Dodger and Oliver jumped off the car just as it skidded off the bridge.

Jenny ran over to Oliver and hugged him.

The next day Fagin and the gang went to Jenny's apartment. Everyone sang "Happy Birthday" as Winston brought out a large cake with eight candles. "Don't forget to make a wish, Jennifer," Winston reminded her.

"The best present I could wish for is in this room—Oliver and all of you, my friends," Jenny declared. The gang barked cheerfully as she blew out the candles.

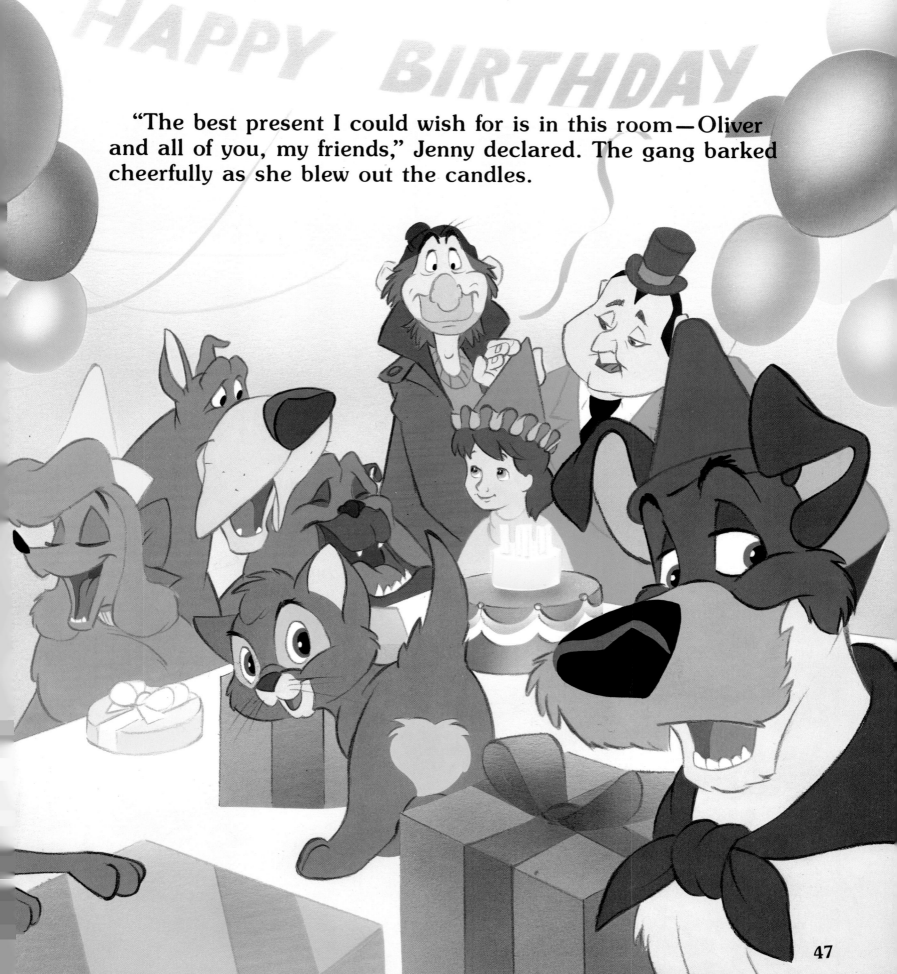

Oliver was very happy living with Jenny. Even Georgette grew fond of him. But Oliver didn't forget his friends, Dodger and the rest of Fagin's gang. Once in a while, he would join them on a stroll through the streets of New York. It was not so frightening a place, now that he had a home.

This edition published in 1988 by
Twin Books
15 Sherwood Place
Greenwich, CT 06830
USA

Copyright © 1988 The Walt Disney Company

Directed by HELENA Productions Ltd.
Image adaptation by Van Gool-Lefevre-Loiseaux

ISBN 0 86124 505 9

Printed in Hong Kong

The Wonderful World of Disney